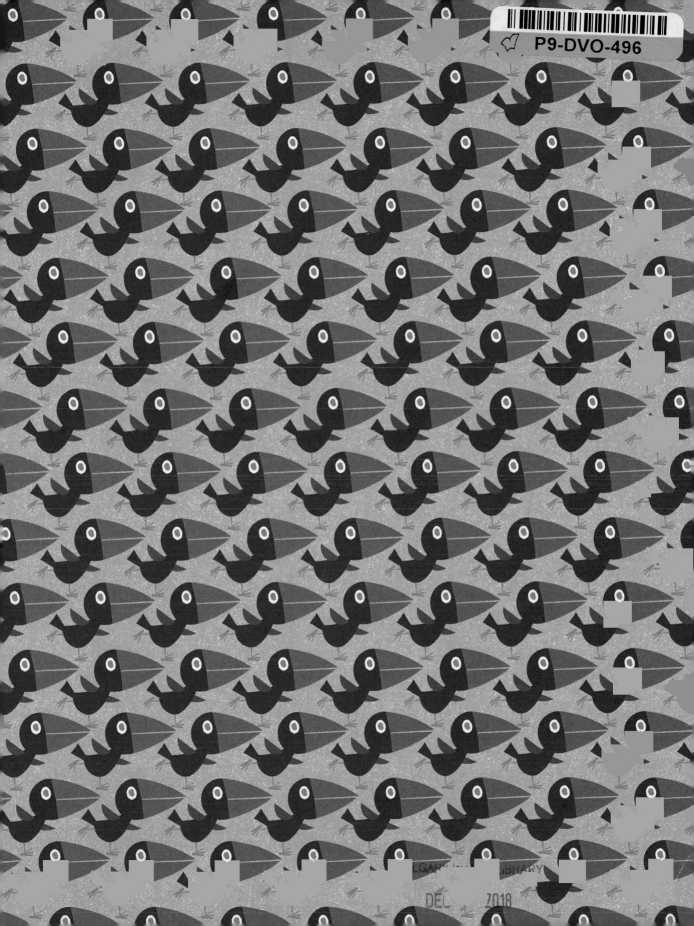

Britta Teckentrup

Oskar
can ...

Prestel
Munich · London · New York

Oskar can jump almost as high as Mo...

...and count to four.

Oskar can do yoga ...

...and make the perfect cup of tea.

Oskar can sing the most beautiful songs...

...and kick his ball as high as the sky.

Oskar can dig the deepest holes...

...and build the highest towers.

His favourite pebble is always on top!

Oskar can fly to Mo all on his own.

Together they can ride their bike.

Oskar can ski ...

...and dance on the ice.

Oskar can almost swim without aids...

...and make the biggest splash!

What can you do?

© 2018, Prestel Verlag, Munich · London · New York
A member of Verlagsgruppe Random House GmbH
Neumarkter Strasse 28 · 81673 Munich

Prestel Publishing Ltd.
14-17 Wells Street
London W1T 3PD

Prestel Publishing
900 Broadway, Suite 603
New York, NY 10003

Editorial direction: Doris Kutschbach
Production management: Astrid Wedemeyer
Typesetting: Anne Swodenk
Printing and binding: TBB, a.s. Banská Bystrica
Paper: Tauro

Verlagsgruppe Random House FSC® N001967

Printed in Slovakia

ISBN 978-3-7913-7270-9
www.prestel.com

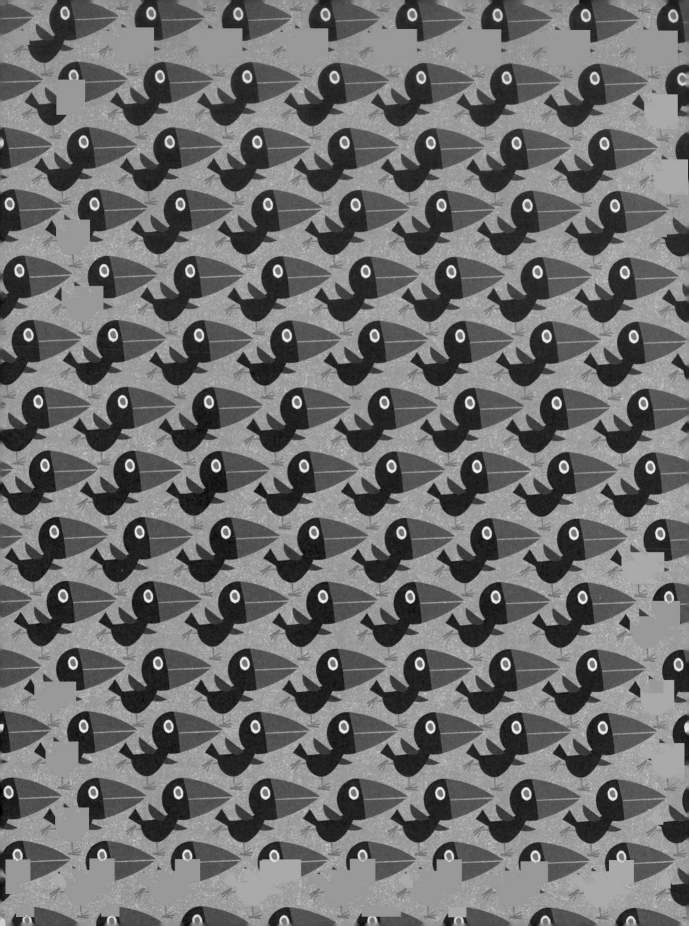